Writing Builders

Ben and Bailey Build a
BOOK REPORT

by Rachel Lynette
illustrated by Randy Chewning

Content Consultant

Jan Lacina, Ph.D., College of Education
Texas Christian University

NORWOOD HOUSE 🏠 PRESS
CHICAGO, ILLINOIS

Norwood House Press
P.O. Box 316598
Chicago, Illinois 60631
For information regarding Norwood House Press, please visit
our website at:
www.norwoodhousepress.com or call 866-565-2900.

Editor: Melissa York
Designer: Emily Love
Project Management: Red Line Editorial

Library of Congress Cataloging-in-Publication Data
Ben and Bailey build a book report / by Rachel Lynette ;
illustrated by Randy Chewning.
    p. cm.
Includes bibliographical references.
Summary: "After school, two friends Ben and Bailey, learn
about writing book reports"--Provided by publisher.
ISBN-13: 978-1-59953-506-7 (library edition : alk. paper)
ISBN-10: 1-59953-506-8 (library edition : alk. paper)
ISBN-13: 978-1-60357-386-3 (e-book : alk. paper)
ISBN-10: 1-60357-386-0 (e-book : alk. paper)
1. Language arts (Elementary) 2. Report writing . 3. English
language Composition and exercises. I. Chewning, Randy, ill.
II. Title.
LB1576.L916 2012
371.3'0281--dc22
                                    2011039359

Manufactured in the United States of America in North
Mankato, Minnesota.
195N—012012

Words in **black bold** are defined in the glossary.

My First Book Report

I love to read. My mom tells everyone I always have my nose in a book. So I should have been thrilled when my teacher said that our class was going to write book reports. But I was totally freaked out! Reading is fun, but writing a report about a book sounds much harder.

Luckily, I go to our neighborhood community center after school. My friend Ben also goes there. He's a year older than me, and he learned how to write a book report last year. He promised to help me today after school. He says a book report is like a sandwich. I like sandwiches, so maybe I'll like book reports too!

By Bailey, age 9

"Hey Bailey, want to play checkers?" Ben asked.

"I wish I could," replied Bailey glumly. "But I have to work on my book report. It's due Friday!"

"Have you started it yet?"

"Not exactly. I read the book, though," said Bailey. "*Lemonade Summer*. It's the report part I'm having trouble with."

"Oh, *Lemonade Summer*," said Ben with a smile. "We read that in school last year. I really liked the part when Lizzy ran out of the house in her pajamas."

"Me too! And there was the part when she accidentally made the lemonade with salt instead of sugar. And there was the traffic jam and then the mayor came and said . . ."

"Wait a minute!" Ben interrupted. "You're out of control! Your ideas are great, but you need to organize them."

"I know I do, but how?"

"I have a good trick for that," added a voice behind them.

Ben and Bailey turned around to see their favorite after-school instructor, Shelly. She came up to their table and placed her sandwich in front of them. "A book report is kind of like a sandwich," Shelly said.

"That's what my teacher said," agreed Ben.

Shelly explained, "You are writing about a **fiction** book, right? A fiction book report starts with an **introduction** and ends with a **conclusion**. Those are like the two pieces of bread. In the middle are the three story elements."

"What are those?" asked Bailey.

"Those are the main parts of a story," said Shelly. "The **setting** is where and when the story takes place. If we were in a story, the setting would be this community center. Then comes the **characters**, the people in the story. That would be the three of us."

"I remember now," said Bailey. "We learned about story elements in school. The last one is the **plot**. If we were in a story, writing the book report would be the plot."

"Exactly," said Shelly. "You can think of the lettuce as the setting, the cheese as the characters, and the meat as the plot."

Shelly picked up her sandwich. "I'm going to go help Andy with his math. Let me know if you need anything else."

"Okay," said Ben. "Let's use the sandwich idea to make a **graphic organizer** for your book report. My teacher said a graphic organizer is a great way to sort out your ideas before you start writing. We won't include every little detail. We just need the important parts."

Ben took a sheet of notebook paper and wrote down the parts of the report. Then Bailey took her pencil and started filling in details from the book. When she was done, she showed it to Ben again.

LEMONADE SUMMER (SANDWICH)
Graphic Organizer

INTRODUCTION (bread)

SETTING (lettuce)
- Lizzy's house and neighborhood in a small town
- Takes place in the summer

CHARACTERS (cheese)
- Lizzy (main character)
- Lizzy's best friend, Laura
- The mayor

PLOT (meat)
- Lizzy opens a lemonade stand
- Hundreds of people come to her stand and cause a traffic jam
- The mayor says she cannot sell lemonade
- Lizzy solves the problem

CONCLUSION (bread)

"See?" said Ben, pointing to the **outline**. "Each part is a paragraph, so the report will be five paragraphs long."

"That sounds like a lot to write," said Bailey, looking concerned.

"You don't have to write it all at the same time," Ben reassured her. "We can work on the introduction now. You can do the setting and the characters at home tonight. I can help you with the plot and the conclusion tomorrow."

"That doesn't sound so bad," said Bailey, picking up her pencil. "Let's get started. I know I need to include the title and the author in the introduction."

This book report is about <u>Lemonade Summer</u> by Lynette Robbins.

"Shelly!" Bailey called, waving. "Can you read my first sentence, please?"

Shelly came back over. "Well, that is okay," she said. "But I think you can do better. You could write about something exciting or interesting from the book. Or you could start with a question."

Bailey erased her first sentence, thought for a few minutes, then started writing again.

"That's great!" said Shelly and Ben together.

Have you ever had a lemonade stand? Lemonade Summer by Lynette Robbins is about the best lemonade stand ever!

Ben looked at the clock.

"My dad should be outside now," he said. "Goodnight, Shelly! Goodnight, Bailey! I will help you more tomorrow if you need it."

"Goodnight, Ben!" chorused Shelly and Bailey.

When Bailey got home, she pulled the outline out of her backpack. The outline said the next part of the report should be about the book's setting. Bailey remembered how Shelly said the setting is the lettuce part of the book report sandwich.

Then she wrote:

Most of <u>Lemonade Summer</u> takes place in Woodinville.

Bailey reread her sentence and thought about what Shelly had said about how she should make her book report interesting. She erased the sentence and wrote:

Most of <u>Lemonade Summer</u> takes place in a quiet neighborhood in Woodinville, a small town.

Bailey checked the book to see if the author had said where Woodinville was, but she hadn't, so Bailey added:

The author does not say where Woodinville is located.

Then Bailey got stuck. She knew that the setting of a book has two parts, where the story takes place and when it takes place. The time of year was in the title, but the author did not say what year it was.

Bailey looked out her bedroom door and saw her mom talking on the telephone. This reminded her that Lizzy called her best friend Laura on a cell phone and that Lizzy sent her friends e-mail. Bailey smiled and began to write again.

She also does not say when the story takes place, but since there are cell phones and computers, it probably takes place in the present time. We know from the title that it takes place in the summer.

Bailey looked at the outline again. The next part of the book report was the characters, or as Shelly would put it, the cheese. That part was easier for Bailey. She wrote a few sentences about Lizzy and then wrote about Lizzy's best friend, Laura.

The main character in <u>Lemonade Summer</u> is Lizzy Merryton. Lizzy is ten years old. She is smart and funny, but she does not always do what she is supposed to. Her best friend is Laura Rundle. Laura is quiet and much more serious than Lizzy. Lizzy and Laura have been best friends since kindergarten.

Bailey thought a little more about the book and decided that the mayor was also an important character. She had just finished writing about him when her mother called her for dinner.

The next day, she showed Ben what she had written. "The author didn't really give a time period, but I figured it out using clues from the book," said Bailey.

"That was clever. I like how you wrote a sentence or two about each of the main characters, too," said Ben. "Now you're ready to write about the plot. You might want to write about every little thing that happened. But that will make your summary long and boring."

"No worries," said Bailey confidently, "I still have my outline. Last night, following the outline kept me focused on the most important parts." Bailey got right to work on the plot while Ben did some of his math homework.

"Hmmmm," said Bailey, looking stumped. "I'm starting the conclusion, and I'm not sure what to write."

"The conclusion is my favorite part!" said Ben. "You get to write your opinions and see how the book is like your own life. You can write about how you felt while you read the book, things the book reminded you of, and whether you would recommend it. You could also write about why you think the author wrote the story and what kind of job he or she did."

"Oh, well, when you put it like that, it does sound fun. I have plenty of opinions about *Lemonade Summer*! It was a good book, but the part with the mayor wasn't very . . ."

"Don't tell me," interrupted Ben, "Write it down!"

Bailey did just that and, before long, her book report was finished!

Lemonade Summer
by Bailey W.

Have you ever had a lemonade stand?
<u>Lemonade Summer</u> by Lynette Robbins is about
the best lemonade stand ever! But it turns out
that being the best can lead to trouble.
   Most of <u>Lemonade Summer</u> takes place
in a quiet neighborhood in Woodinville, a small
town. The author does not say where Woodinville
is located. She also does not say when the story
takes place, but since there are cell phones and
computers, it probably takes place in the present
time. We know from the title that it takes place in
the summer.
   The main character in <u>Lemonade Summer</u>
is Lizzy Merryton. Lizzy is ten years old. She
is smart and funny, but she does not always do
what she is supposed to. Her best friend is Laura
Rundle. Laura is quiet and much more serious
than Lizzy. Lizzy and Laura have been best
friends since kindergarten. Another important
character is the mayor of Wooodinville. The mayor
is not a very nice man. He is always in a hurry
and does not seem to like children very much.
Also, he hates lemonade!

The story begins when Lizzy's grandma sends her a recipe for lemonade. Lizzy and Laura decide to open a lemonade stand in front of Lizzy's house. The lemonade is so good that before long there are hundreds of people waiting in line to get some, causing a huge traffic jam on their street. The mayor shuts down the lemonade stand because of the traffic jam. Lizzy and Laura are sad until Lizzy gets a great idea. That night, she and Laura e-mail the recipe to all of their friends. The next day there are lemonade stands all over the town and everyone who wants the yummy lemonade can get some without causing huge traffic jams.

I liked <u>Lemonade Summer</u> because it was funny and because Lizzy came up with such a creative way to solve the problem. But I don't think this story is very realistic. I don't think any lemonade stand could cause a big traffic jam. I would still recommend this book though because it made me laugh and because I really like the way the author made Lizzy such an interesting character.

"That's great!" said Ben. "This makes me want to read *Lemonade Summer* again."

"Thanks!" smiled Bailey. "All that writing was thirsty work. I hope Shelly will bring us some lemonade!"

You Can Write a Book Report, Too!

A book report is a great way to show what you have learned from reading a book. It is a good idea to take notes about your book while you are reading it. Write down important points that you might need later when you are writing the report. Be sure to write down the page number where you found each point!

Writing a book report is not hard as long as you stay organized. Writing a graphic organizer can really help. Remember, a fiction book report has five main parts: the introduction, the setting, the main characters, the plot, and the conclusion. Here are some notes that Bailey wrote to help for her next book report:

Introduction: Attention-getting first sentence and the title and author of the book.

Setting: Where and when the book takes place.

Characters: Two to four main characters with short descriptions.

Plot: Summary of the story—important parts only!

Conclusion: Opinions and feelings about the book. Also a recommendation.

After you have written your outline, you are ready to start writing your report. Remember to include only the important points. While you are writing your report, you may want to ask yourself, "Is this part important to the story or is it just an interesting detail?" If you get tired, it is okay to stop for a while. You may want to write your report in two or three sittings.

Make sure you correct any spelling or grammar errors before you turn in your report. One thing that can help is to read your report out loud. You may even want to read it to a friend or a family member.

Glossary

characters: the people in a story.

conclusion: tells your readers what they just read, and leaves them thinking about what you wrote.

fiction: a story or book that is not true.

graphic organizer: a visual way to put your thoughts in order such as an outline or a list.

introduction: tells your readers what they are about to read.

outline: an organized list showing the main points of a piece of writing.

plot: the events that make up the story.

setting: the place and time where a story takes place.

For More Information

Books

Norris, Jill. *How to Report on Books, Grades 3-4*, Monterey, CA: Evan-Moor, 2009.

Williams, Rozanne Lanczak. *Writing about Books*, Huntington Beach, CA: Creative Teaching Press, 2006.

Websites

The Book Report
http://www.lkwdpl.org/study/bookrep/

This website features a step by step guide to writing a book report.

Book Report Now!
http://www.randomhouse.com/kids/bookreportnow/

This guide to writing a book report includes several creative approaches.

Book Report Sandwich Station
http://www.scholastic.com/kids/homework/sandwich.asp

Fill in the blanks to make a book report using a sandwich format.

About the Author

Rachel Lynette has written more than 100 books for children of all ages as well as resource materials for teachers. When she isn't writing she enjoys spending time with her family and friends, traveling, reading, drawing, crocheting colorful hats, biking, and playing racquetball.